MW00980136

Corvettes

ERIC ETHAN

Gareth Stevens Publishing
MILWAUKEE

For a free color catalog describing Gareth Stevens Publishing's list of high-quality books and multimedia programs, call 1-800-542-2595 (USA) or 1-800-461-9120 (Canada). Gareth Stevens Publishing's Fax: (414) 225-0377.
See our catalog, too, on the World Wide Web: http://gsinc.com

Library of Congress Cataloging-in-Publication Data

Ethan, Eric.
Corvettes / by Eric Ethan.
p. cm. — (Great American muscle cars—an imagination library series.
Includes index.
Summary: Surveys the history of the Corvette and its designs, engines, performance, and costs.
ISBN 0-8368-1744-3 (lib. bdg.)
1. Corvette automobile—Juvenile literature. [1. Corvette automobile.] I. Title. II. Series: Ethan, Eric. Great American muscle cars—an imagination library series.
TL215.C6E84 1998
629.222'2—dc21 97-41186

First published in North America in 1998 by
Gareth Stevens Publishing
1555 North RiverCenter Drive, Suite 201
Milwaukee, WI 53212 USA

Text: Eric Ethan
Page layout: Eric Ethan, Helene Feider
Cover design: Helene Feider
Series design: Shari Tikus

Printed in the United States of America

1 2 3 4 5 6 7 8 9 02 01 00 99 98

TABLE OF CONTENTS

Words that appear in the glossary are printed in **boldface** type the first time they occur in the text.

THE FIRST CORVETTE

The first Corvette rolled off the assembly line in 1953. It is the oldest American muscle car. *Corvettes* were named after small, agile warships that chased submarines during World War II. The **design** was the idea of Harley Earl, an **engineer** for General Motors.

Earl believed American car buyers wanted a basic sports car that might not be very fast but was fun to drive. This was a big gamble for General Motors. In Europe, small sports cars like the Corvette were very popular, but most Americans were not familiar with them. People were slow to accept the Corvette. But eventually, Earl's design paid off.

Muscle cars, like the Corvette, are American-made, two-door sports ***coupes*** *with powerful engines made for high-performance driving. This 1958 Corvette shows the European round fender styling common during the first five years that Corvettes were made.*

Diner
DINER
BE HAPPY
1856
California
3JET415

WHAT DO CORVETTES LOOK LIKE?

The first Corvettes looked very much like the 1958 model pictured on the previous page. They had smooth lines and a large **grill**. They were similar to the MG and Austin Healey, two-seat English sports cars of the time.

In 1963, Corvette entered the muscle car era and came out with an all-new **angular** design. The Stingray and Mako Shark models offered larger engines and better handling at high speed. The 1963 design still can be seen in Corvettes built today. All Corvettes have one thing in common. Their bodies are made of GRP — glass reinforced plastic, or fiberglass. No other American car bodies are made completely of fiberglass.

The 1967 Stingray Coupe is one of the most popular styles among Corvette collectors.

WHAT WAS THE FASTEST CORVETTE?

The original Corvettes were not designed to go very fast. They were quick and fun but did not reach top speeds. In the muscle car era of the 1960s, however, speed became important, and General Motors redesigned the Corvette for speed.

By 1967, Corvettes were as fast as any other general production car. The 1967 Stingray carried a powerful 427-cubic-inch (7-liter) engine. The greater the cubic inches, the more **horsepower** an engine can create. By 1968, an even more powerful motor, the L-88, could be ordered. It was so powerful that General Motors would not put a radio or heater in the car — this Corvette was strictly for the racetrack.

The 1967 Corvette Stingray with a 427-cubic-inch (7-liter) engine produced 400 horsepower.

CORVETTE ENGINES

Engines in even high-performance motors in the Corvette had a very simple look. The 1965 Turbo Jet motor shown here could produce over 425 horsepower. It was one of the most powerful motors made during the 1960s. With this motor, Corvettes could easily reach speeds over 100 miles (160 kilometers) per hour.

While high-performance engines of the past were simple in design, they had their bad points. They used a large amount of gasoline and caused air **pollution**. Special equipment on modern car engines has improved gas mileage and reduced pollution.

A 1965 Corvette Stingray 396-cubic-inch (6.5-liter) engine.

TURBO-JET 425 HP
396

CORVETTE INTERIORS

The Corvette passenger compartment was small compared to those in full-size **sedans** of the 1960s. It had room for two bucket seats and a center console **stick shift**. The driver's and passenger's legs extended well under the dashboard. The car was low to the ground, similar to European sports cars.

A complete set of **gauges** and instruments was standard equipment on most Corvettes. Gauges indicate speed and how a high-performance engine is operating.

The passenger compartment of a 1965 Corvette Stingray.

CORVETTES RACING

A Corvette with a large engine was almost too powerful for the car's **frame**. Special handling equipment had to be added to the road racing version of the car to improve its safety.

The Chevrolet division of General Motors sponsored racing teams during the 1960s. These teams raced Corvettes, such as the Grand Sport pictured. The Grand Sport had a **tubular** frame, a huge 427-cubic-inch (7-liter) engine, special **carburetors**, and more power than most drivers could handle. These Corvettes could easily reach 140 miles (225 km) per hour. Above that speed, the front end would lift dangerously off the ground. The upper limit of the lightweight Corvette body design was reached with the Grand Sport.

The 1963 Corvette Grand Sport was one of the fastest road race cars of the 1960s.

BEAUTIFUL CORVETTES

Many Corvette fans believe the first Corvette design in the 1950s was a **classic**. They feel the muscle car designs of the mid-1960s lost much of the original style.

The 1962 Corvette was the final year of the original design. It was the first model to sell ten thousand units that year, a low number considering how popular the car was. Most larger sedans sold over one hundred thousand units each year. Early Corvettes lacked comfort features that buyers looked for. Besides having only two seats, early Corvettes had no heaters. The ride was uncomfortable, and the cars were noisy. But this did not stop fans of the Corvette from thinking Corvettes were the most beautiful cars ever made.

Corvette's 1962 convertible presented classic styling during the original design's final year.

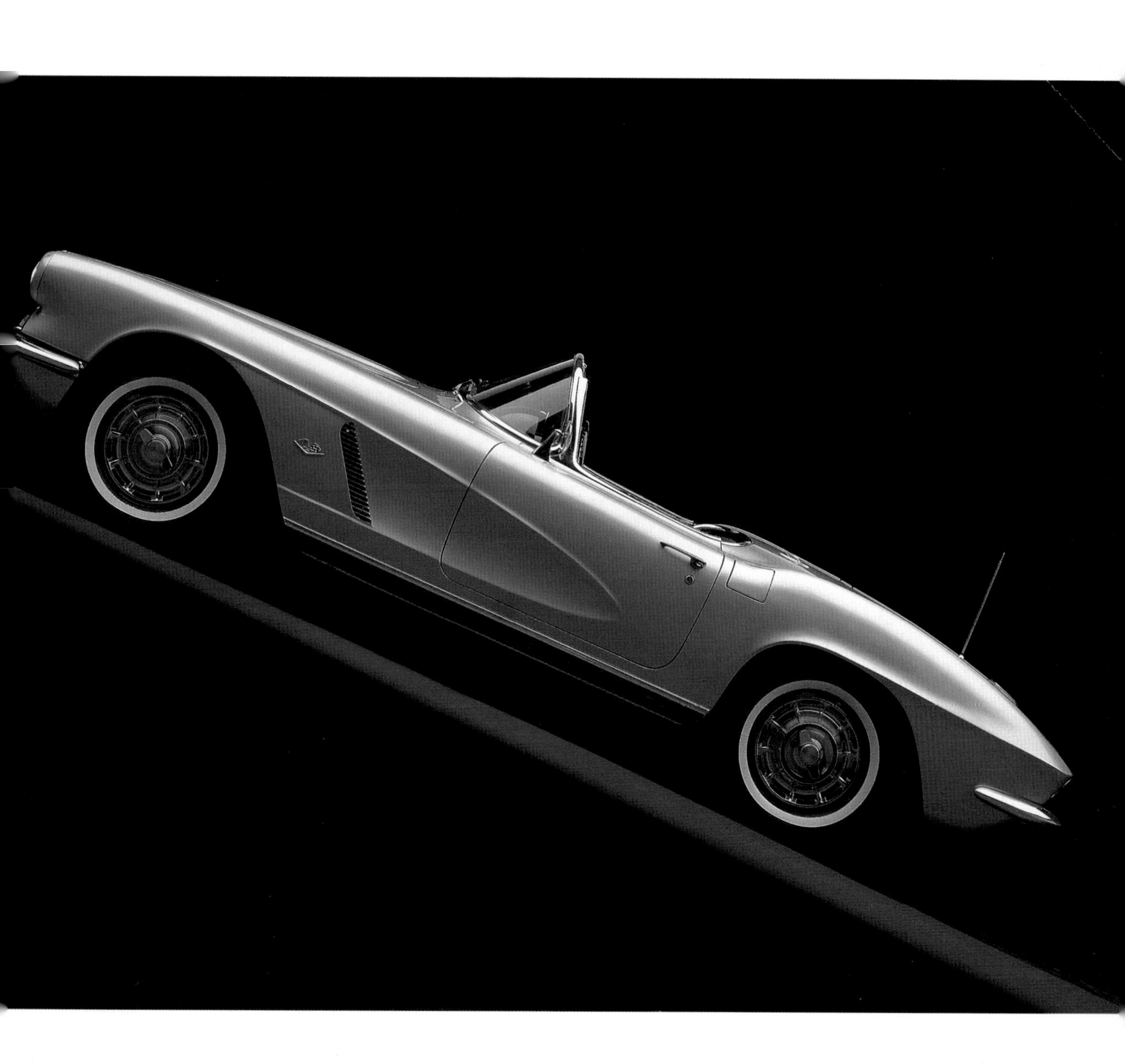

TODAY'S CORVETTES

Corvettes are one of the few muscle cars to survive the 1960s, and they are still made today. They are manufactured near Bowling Green, Kentucky.

In 1991, the ZR-1 model was introduced. It produced 375 horsepower and was close to the fastest production car in the world. But all this speed comes at a price. A new ZR-1 model costs over $50,000, nearly twenty times the price of a 1953 model.

The 1992 Corvette pictured has a smaller engine and lower top speed than earlier models, but it is still very fast. The new Corvettes are made of fiberglass, as always. They get far better gas mileage and are not as polluting as earlier versions.

Modern Corvettes have retained the basic sports car design that made them popular in the 1960s.

WHAT DID ORIGINAL CORVETTES COST?

The very first Corvettes in 1953 cost about $2,500. Prices did not increase very much over the next ten years. But by the peak of the muscle car era, Corvettes with all the power **options** cost about $5,000. This made them an expensive car for that time. Mustangs, Camaros, and Firebirds generally cost about half that.

By 1963, the Corvette had been around quite a while. It had a small, but loyal, following. People who liked Corvettes were willing to pay more to have one.

The 1963 Corvette Stingray split window coupe is considered one of the most beautiful and collectible of all the Corvettes from the 1960s.

CALIFORNIA
PARK PERFORMANCE
CORVETTES

PLACES TO WRITE

Vette
McMullen and Argus Publishing
774 South Placentia Avenue
Placentia, CA 92870-6832

National Corvette Museum
350 Corvette Drive
P.O. Box 1953
Bowling Green, KY 42102-1953

National Corvette Owners Association
P.O. Box 16050
Falls Church, VA 22040

Classic Motorbooks
729 Prospect Avenue
P. O. Box 1
Osceola, WI 54020
1-800-826-6600

INDEX